SCOOBY-DOO! KEEPAWAY CAMP ™

By Sonia Sander
Illustrated by Scott Gross

ISBN 978-0-545-82611-2

10 9 8 7 6 5 4 3 2 1   15 16 17 18 19/0

Printed in the U.S.A.   40

First printing July 2015

SCHOLASTIC INC.

It was the first day of summer.

The kids from Mystery, Inc. were on the way to Fred's old camp.

"Let's go, gang!" called Fred.

"Like, ready when you are," said Shaggy.

A few hours later, the Mystery Machine sped up the camp's driveway.

"Jeepers, this place looks empty," said Daphne.

"The owner, Jasper, told me the camp needs work," Fred said.

SLEEPAWAY CAMP

"Welcome back, Fred!" said Jasper. He gave the gang tents and sleeping bags. "Just like the old days, right?"

Daphne nodded as dust flew off her tent.

"You can stay in our best campsite," said
Jasper. "I asked Hank to clean it up for you."

Hank was pushing a wheelbarrow filled
with rocks.

"We had a lot of rockslides this winter,"
Jasper told the gang.

Scooby and Shaggy started setting up their tent.

"Ruh-roh!" cried Scooby. The tent fell down on him and Shaggy!

"Like, this one's broken," said Shaggy.

"You just forgot a pole," said Velma.

That night, Jasper and the gang sat around the campfire.

"No one comes here anymore," said Jasper. "People believe the legend of Bigfoot."

"Bigfoot?" Scooby asked. "Rhat's that?"

"A wild ape-man," Jasper explained.

"People have seen his giant footprints," Jasper went on. "He hides during the day. At night, he goes out to look for food."

"Yikes!" cried Shaggy. "We better keep our snacks safe, right, Scoob?"

"Right!" said Scooby.

Back in their tent, Scooby and Shaggy made funny shadows on the wall.

"Like, check out my rabbit," said Shaggy.

"Rool, Raggy," said Scooby.

That night, there was a big storm. It woke up
Shaggy and Scooby.
Crash! Bam! Boom!
Their tent began to leak.

"Listen," said Shaggy. "It stopped raining."
He peeked out of the tent flap. "Yikes, Scoob.
What is that?"

A dark figure loomed outside the tent.

"*RAAHHHH!*" cried the creature. It ripped
open the tent flap.

"Rigfoot!" cried Scooby.

"Like, run, Scoob!" Shaggy shouted.

Scooby and Shaggy's shouts woke up Fred, Daphne, and Velma.

"Look out, gang!" cried Shaggy. "Bigfoot is after us!"

Bigfoot chased the gang all the way to the edge of the woods.

Then it started to rain again. Bigfoot ran back into the woods.

"Looks like he's giving up," said Fred.

"Maybe he's afraid to get wet," said Velma.

The next morning, the gang told Jasper about Bigfoot.

"If we follow the tracks, we'll find the monster," said Fred.

"Like, count us out!" said Shaggy.

"Would you do it for a Scooby Snack?" asked Daphne.

A few Scooby Snacks later, Scooby and Shaggy were following Bigfoot's tracks.

"The trail leads into the woods," said Fred. "Follow me!"

"There's a cave up ahead," Fred said.
Velma looked at the footprints. "It looks like
Bigfoot headed that way."

The tracks led to the cave door.
"Jinkies!" said Velma. "It's all boarded up."
"Like, let's obey the sign," said Shaggy.
"Reah, ret's ro!" said Scooby.

"Let's take a quick look inside," said Fred.
The gang's flashlights lit up the dark cave.
Inside, paint cans and rocks lay all over the floor.
"Jeepers," said Daphne. "What a mess!"

The gang started looking for clues.
Then Hank appeared.
"What are you kids doing here?" he yelled.
"Scram before you get into trouble!"

The gang hurried back to camp. A big truck was parked near the toolshed.

"That's weird. Let's take a look," said Fred. The truck was full of rocks!

Daphne spotted a clue on the ground. "Look how this rock sparkles," she said.

"That's not a rock," said Velma. "It's a diamond painted to *look* like a rock!"

Suddenly, Bigfoot appeared. "*RAAHH!*" it cried.
The kids ran away.
"C'mon, guys, let's hide in the shed," Fred said.
"Looks like we lost him," said Shaggy.

The gang looked around the shed.

"Here's an axe and a pick," said Daphne.

"For mining diamonds," said Velma.

"It's time to find out who Bigfoot really is," said Fred. "Scooby and Shaggy, we're going to need your help."

As usual, Scooby and Shaggy were the bait in Fred's plan.

The two buddies stole some rocks from the cave.

Soon, Bigfoot was chasing them again.

"Like, head for the lake, Scoob!" Shaggy cried.

Fred, Velma, and Daphne were waiting by the shore.

Scooby and Shaggy hopped across a long row of boats.

They raced toward the water park.

"*RAHHHH!*" Bigfoot growled as it chased them. Fred, Velma, and Daphne began the next part of the plan.

Bigfoot followed Scooby and Shaggy up the ladder of the waterslide.

When it got to the top, it was trapped!

There was nowhere to go but down.

SPLASH!

The water washed off Bigfoot's disguise.
It was Hank!

"You found a diamond mine in the cave on Jasper's land," said Velma.

"And you decided to keep the diamonds," said Daphne.

"I was going to be rich," said Hank, "if it weren't for you meddling kids!"

"I'll use the money from the mine to fix up this old camp," Jasper said. "Thanks, kids!"

The Mystery, Inc. finally got to relax.

"Like Scoob, this is the life!" Shaggy said.

"Ruh-huh!" barked Scooby. "Scooby-Dooby-Doo!"